The
SPOOKY
HALLOWEEN
PARTY

by Annabelle Prager
pictures by Tomie de Paola

An I AM READING *Book*

Pantheon Books

To the trick-or-treaters in *my* apartment house
who are never too big to be scared on Halloween.

Copyright © 1981 by Annabelle Prager
Illustrations Copyright © 1981 by Tomie de Paola
All rights reserved under International and Pan-American
Copyright Conventions. Published in the United States by
Pantheon Books, a division of Random House, Inc.,
New York, and simultaneously in Canada by
Random House of Canada Limited, Toronto.
Manufactured in the United States of America
10   9   8   7

Library of Congress Cataloging in Publication Data
Prager, Annabelle. The spooky Halloween party.
(AN *I Am Reading* BOOK)
Summary: Albert doesn't recognize anyone
at Nicky's Halloween party,
even when they take off their masks.
[1. Halloween—Fiction.   2. Parties—Fiction]
I. De Paola, Tomie.   II. Title.   III. Series: I am reading book.
PZ7.P8864Sp 1981   [E]   81-1945
ISBN 0-394-84370-3   AACR2
ISBN 0-394-94370-8 (lib. bdg.)

The
SPOOKY
HALLOWEEN
PARTY

One

"*Whoo whoo whoo*," said Nicky.

"Why are you asking me *who*?" said Albert.

"I'm not asking you who," said Nicky.

"I'm getting ready

to scare everybody on Halloween."

"What are you going to do
on Halloween?" asked Albert.
"Didn't I tell you?" said Nicky.
"I'm going to have
a very spooky Halloween party
at my new apartment house.

Everybody is going to be scared
out of their wits."
"Like who?" said Albert.
"Like you and Jan,
my cousin Suzanne,
and Morris and Doris
and Dan," said Nicky.
"Getting scared on Halloween
is for little kids," said Albert.
"Nothing is going to scare me."
"That's what you think," said Nicky.

"What are *you* going to be
on Halloween?" said Albert.
"I can't tell you," said Nicky.
"Nobody should know
who anybody is till after we've gone
trick-or-treating.
That way it will be very spooky
and we can all scare each other."
"Nobody is going to scare me,"
said Albert.
"I'll know who everybody is
right away."
"We'll see about that," said Nicky.

TWO

Albert went home
to think of a good Halloween costume.
"Nicky thinks he's so smart,"
said Albert.
"But all he has to do
is go *whoo whoo whoo*
and I'll know him right away."

Ring-a-ding-ding, the phone rang.

It was Jan.

"Will you lend me your mop
for Nicky's spooky Halloween party?"
said Jan.

"I have a good idea for a costume.
You'll never guess who I am."

"I have a good idea too," said Albert.

"But I haven't got a mop."

He hung up.

"I'll bet Jan
is going to be a witch,"
thought Albert.
"And she thinks that
witches ride on mops.
How dumb can she be?"

Ring-a-ding-ding.

The phone rang again.

This time it was Dan.

"Guess what?" said Dan.

"Nicky invited me

to his spooky Halloween party,

and I'm going to be a pirate!"

"You're not supposed to tell
what you're going to be," said Albert.
"Why not?" asked Dan.
"Because now I'll know who you are,"
said Albert.
"But you already know who I am,"
said Dan.
"Oh Dan," said Albert,
"you never get the point,"
and he hung up.

Albert got out the box of old clothes.
"I'm sick of the clothes
in this box," he said.
"I've worn them all before.

I know, this year I'll wear the box!
I'll be a robot.
Nobody will know it's me.
We'll see who is going to scare who
at Nicky's spooky Halloween party."

Three

On Halloween Albert set out

for Nicky's new apartment house.

He was wearing the box upside down.

All you could see of Albert

were his arms and legs.

He practiced talking

in a squeaky robot voice.

"Where is Nicky's party?"
Albert asked the doorman
at Nicky's new apartment house.
"Take the elevator to the fifth floor.
It's apartment C," said the doorman.
A princess wearing a gold crown
and a big pair of high heel shoes
got in the elevator too.
She pushed button number five.
"She must be Nicky's cousin Suzanne,"
thought Albert.

"You're not very scary,"
Albert said to the princess.
"I'd rather be pretty,"
said the princess.
"Are you going
to the spooky Halloween party?"
"Of course," said Albert.
"Then you can come with me,"
said the princess,
"so the spooks won't get me."
"Don't be silly," said Albert.
"There aren't any spooks."

The elevator stopped at five.

A ghost and a monster

were running up and down the hall.

"It's this way," said the princess.

Albert followed the princess

around a corner.

They stopped at an open door.

"Hey, look at the robot," said a voice.

"Who could it be?"

Albert felt very good.

"I'll know them," he thought,

"But they won't know me!"

Four

It was really spooky at the party.
The only light came from
three little pumpkins.
"Nicky thinks
he can scare everybody,
just because it's dark," Albert said.
"But he can't scare me."
Albert looked around for Nicky.
Was he the owl flapping his wings?
Or was Nicky the goblin
with the stocking over his head?
And which witch was JAN?
The one with the broom
or the one with the shopping bag?

"I know," thought Albert.

"The witch with the broom is Jan.

Somebody must have told her

that witches don't ride on mops."

He went up to the witch

and gave her broom a shake.

"Where's your mop?" said Albert

in his squeaky robot voice.

"Go away or I'll bite you,"

said the witch.

Albert went away.

"What's the matter with Jan?"

he wondered.

He went up to the other witch.

"You better watch out!"

she hissed in a witch's voice.

"The terrible spooks have cast a spell

on everyone here!"

"They HAVE NOT!" said Albert.

"Wait and see," hissed the witch.

Albert decided to find Dan.

But there were no little pirates

anywhere.

Albert felt a tap on his box.

"It's me," said the princess.

"And I'm scared."

"I'M NOT," said Albert.

Just then the goblin shouted,

"Okay you guys.

Time to trick-or-treat.

Head for the stairs."

"That goblin sounds bossy,"

thought Albert, "just like Nicky.

And he thought he could fool me."

Five

Everybody headed for the stairs.

Albert tried to keep up

with the goblin and the owl,

but it was hard to run wearing a box.

And the princess kept losing

her high heel shoes.

So Albert and the princess

had to ring doorbells together.

By the time they reached

the bottom floor

their bags were heavy with treats.

Then Albert and the princess

climbed back up

the long, lonely stairs.

Black shadows waited at every turn.

Way above them a door went *bang!*

"Whoo whoo whoo!"

went a faraway voice.

"Help, a spook!"

yelled the princess.

She grabbed Albert so hard
he almost fell down the stairs.
"That's not a spook!
It's Nicky!" cried Albert.

"Now I know Nicky is the owl.

That's why he keeps hooting!"

"You don't know anything,"

said the princess.

"Even I know who the owl is."

Suddenly a shiver went down Albert.

"Why don't I know who anybody is?"

he thought.

"Maybe I *am* under a spell."

"It's Halloween

and the spooks are going to get us!"

shouted the princess.

"Let's get out of here!"

"Yes, let's!" Albert shouted back.

Six

When Albert and the princess

got back to the party,

Albert's heart was going

thump, thump! thump, thump!

Everybody was waiting in the dark.

"Take off your masks,"
said the bossy goblin.
"I'll turn on the lights."
Albert felt better.
Now he would see his friends.

He looked around for Nicky.

The owl was holding

his mask in his hand.

The owl wasn't Nicky.

The goblin pulled

the stocking off his head.

The goblin wasn't Nicky either.

And who were the witches?

Albert had never seen

either of them before.

In fact, Albert had never seen

anybody at the party before.

Everyone stared at him.

His heart started to thump again.

His knees began to shake.

"There really are spooks," said Albert.

"Spooks have changed my friends
into strangers!"

Seven

Just then the doorbell rang.

"Whoo whoo whoo," went a voice.

"Trick or treat!"

The doorway was full of people.

One was a little pirate

with a patch over his eye.

One was a clown

with hair that looked like a mop.

And one was a ghost with a light

that went on and off.

"Whoo who whooo," said the ghost

flashing his light.

"Whoooo can I scare?"

"Look, there's Albert!"

shouted the little pirate.

"Hey Albert, why didn't you come

to Nicky's Halloween party?"

Albert was all mixed up.

"I did come

to Nicky's Halloween party," he said.

"I am at Nicky's Halloween party.

Aren't I?"

"No, you're at *my* Halloween party,"

said the goblin.

"Nicky's party is around the corner

in Apartment C."

"So there aren't any spooks,

after all," said Albert.

"I'm just at the wrong party!"

Eight

"Now you have to come
to the right party," said the ghost
in Nicky's bossy voice.
"Everybody has to come to my party.
I've got popcorn to eat
and lots of spooky games to play.

So the right party
and the wrong party
ended in a double Halloween party
at Nicky's house
in apartment C.
They played Nicky's spooky games
and screamed and yelled
until their throats were sore.

Finally it was time to go home.
"This was a super special Halloween
even though it was so scary,"
said the princess.

"This was a super special Halloween
just *because* it was so scary,"
said Nicky.
And everyone agreed—even Albert.

ANNABELLE PRAGER was born in New York City and graduated from Sweet Briar College. She then studied at the Yale School of Fine Arts and the Art Students League, and was an illustrator for many years before she wrote her first book for children, THE SURPRISE PARTY, which met with immediate success. She lives with her husband and their two children in Manhattan.

TOMIE DE PAOLA was born in Meriden, Connecticut and graduated from Pratt Institute and the California College of Arts and Crafts. He is very well known for the many books he has written and illustrated for children, including STREGA NONA, a Caldecott Honor Book. He lives in a one hundred and fifty year old farmhouse in New Hampshire.